Dedication

To the wild nights, the stolen moments, and the laughter that echoed through hostel halls.

To the mischievous adventures, the secret crushes, and the love stories that bloomed when we least expected.

To the bonds that were forged over midnight snacks, shared dreams, and endless conversations — friendships that turned into family.

This book is for the unforgettable days that shaped us, the memories that we'll carry forever, and the lifelong friends who made every moment worth it.

Here is to hostel life and love – a chapter in time that will always be written on our hearts.

Contents

WHISPERS OF SHOOTING STARS

A JOURNEY OF REDISCOVERY

KEYA SRIRAM

ISBN
Paperback 979-8-89632-309-9
Hardcase 979-8-89699-359-9

CHAPTER 1

STARS OVER NUBRA VALLEY

*K*ia lay outside her tent, her arms folded beneath her head, gazing up at the endless stretch of stars flickering across the dark night sky. A shooting star streaked across the sky, and she smiled, letting out a soft sigh. The cold, crisp air of Nubra Valley in Leh Ladakh wrapped around her, but the chill didn't bother her. She felt strangely at peace as if the mountains themselves were whispering secrets to her soul. Her Bullet motorbike stood a few feet away, its chrome gleaming under the moonlight. It had been a long, exhilarating ride to get here—through winding mountain passes, rivers, and remote villages. But now, in the stillness of the night, she had finally found what she had been searching for.

Kia had come a long way, both literally and metaphorically. She had been running for years, from home, from heartbreak, and even from herself. The stars twinkled as if they knew the truth, but tonight, Kia wasn't thinking about the past. She was just here, in this moment, allowing herself to breathe freely under the vast Ladakh sky.

Memories flashed through her mind as she lay there, her eyes growing heavy with fatigue and serenity. A small smile played on her lips as she remembered the family that had raised her, the hostel she had once called home, and the adventures that had shaped her into the woman she is today.

CHAPTER 2

THE SHARMA FAMILY CIRCUS

*L*ife in the Sharma household was anything but quiet. Kia was the heartbeat of the family—bubbly, mischievous, and impossible to contain. The Sharma's lived in a sprawling ancestral home in Assam, surrounded by lush green fields and a close-knit community. Her father, Mr. Sharma, a government officer, was a man of few words but had a soft spot for his daughter's shenanigans. Her mother, Mrs. Sharma, was the quintessential homemaker, forever fussing over her children with warm food and loving scolds.

And then there was Kia's younger brother, Kunal. Despite being three years younger, Kunal was far more mature than Kia. He was calm, collected, and often the voice of reason in their sibling duo. But that didn't stop him from indulging in Kia's endless schemes. From sneaking out late at night to climb the neighbor's guava tree to stealing ice cream from the kitchen while their mother was out shopping, the two of them were inseparable.

Though Kunal was always the more sensible one, Kia was the one who breathed life into every corner of the house. Everyone loved her—the neighbors, the shopkeepers, and even the strictest of her teachers couldn't help but crack a smile when Kia's mischievous grin lit up a room. She was a whirlwind of energy, the kind of girl who could talk her way out of trouble and leave behind only laughter in her wake.

Despite her antics, Kia excelled in school. Her love for sports and her sharp wit made her popular among her peers, and her teachers admired her curiosity and passion for learning. But, underneath all the fun and chaos, Kia carried restlessness inside her, a desire to explore life beyond the boundaries of her small town.

It wasn't long before that restlessness led her to the next chapter of her life – a decision that would take her far away from the comforts of home and thrust her into the wild and unpredictable world of hostel life.

CHAPTER 3

THE HOSTEL CHRONICLES

*M*oving to the hostel for class 11 was a monumental shift for Kia. Her parents believed the structured environment would instill a sense of discipline in their adventurous daughter. But for Kia, it was less about discipline and more about the prospect of new adventures waiting behind the imposing ivy-covered walls of the hostel.

The day Kia arrived at the hostel, she felt a mix of excitement and nervousness. The hostel building was an imposing structure with ivy-covered walls and long, echoing hallways. As she walked through the gates with her bags, she was greeted by the sight of girls huddled together, exchanging nervous glances. Some were first timers like her, while others were returning for their final two years of school.

Kia soon found herself bonding with a group of equally spirited girls—Priyanka, Rahi, and Sangita. Each one brought her own flavor to the gang. Rahi, bold and unapologetic; Priyanka, the calm mediator; and Sangita, another die-hard Shah Rukh Khan fan who could talk endlessly about Bollywood with Kia. By nightfall, they had all settled into the rhythm of hostel life, though there was one more initiation to go—the infamous yet light-hearted ragging. Ragging in their hostel was a rite of passage—light-hearted and more about bonding than actual bullying.

After the dorm lights were switched off and hostel warden Mr Pachakili Perumal completed his rounds, Kia stood like a self-appointed leader in the middle of the room. "Alright, everyone up!" she whispered fiercely, pulling the covers off her giggling roommates. The ritual began, and each girl was assigned a task.

Rahi, known for her brazen attitude, had to kiss another girl on the lips. The room exploded into pearls of laughter when she finally blushed through it. Chandra, the shy one, imitated Sir Pachakili Perumal's strict Malabari accent, sending everyone into fits of giggles. But the highlight of the night came when it was Sangita's turn.

With a torch in hand, Sangita was tasked to channel her inner Shah Rukh Khan. She held the torch high and began delivering dramatic dialogues in her best SRK voice. *"Main hoon na!"* she exclaimed, chest puffed out like the King Khan himself. But as her voice echoed through the room, the door creaked open ominously. *"Kaun hai be?"* she shouted, still in character, only for the torchlight to reveal none other than our warden, Mr. Pachakili Perumal, standing in the doorway, his face stern and disapproving.

The room froze.

"All of you! Kneel down right now!" Mr. Perumal's voice sliced through the room. Sangita's torch flickered and went out as she dropped it in shock. The entire room burst into a mix of giggles and horror as Sangita spent the rest of the night on her knees, much to everyone's suppressed laughter.

But that was just the beginning of their mischief.

The next day was no less eventful. In class 11, Kia and her friends endured the usual round of introductions. When it was Amit's turn, nerves got the better of him. "Hi, I'm... Kanpur from Amit!" he stammered. The class erupted in laughter. Even Kia, who had been trying to stay serious, couldn't hold back her giggles.

And so, the legend of 'Kanpur Amit' was born.

But as much as life in the hostel seemed like it would settle into a rhythm, new mischief was always brewing. Like the time they discovered a unique way to bypass the strict no-going-outside rule. Weekends meant craving street food, and what could be better than pani puri?

Sangita came up with a genius plan. Instead of sneaking out, they would order pani puri by dangling mugs tied to a rope out of their windows. They stuffed notes inside the mugs for the street vendors, who, understanding the silent plea, filled them with spicy, tangy pani puri. The girls would pull the mugs up, filled with their delicious contraband. The thrill of not getting caught made the snack taste even better.

One particular weekend, though, the antics hit a new level. Kia, in a fit of creativity, decided to prank Sangita, her partner in crime. Inspired by their most recent biology class, Kia spent an evening collecting mosquito blood—yes, real mosquito blood—squished onto paper, crafting a love letter addressed to Sangita. The note read:

"Dear Sangita,

My blood is your blood now.

Will you be mine?

Forever,

Your Secret Admirer"

When Sangita unfolded the letter and realized what the red smudges were, she screamed loudly enough to shake the building. Everyone around burst into uncontrollable laughter, and Sangita, while initially horrified, couldn't help but laugh at the ridiculousness of it all. Kia had managed to terrify and amuse her in equal measure.

But not every night was full of pranks and jokes. Once a month, the entire hostel gathered for a mandatory movie night. It was supposed to be a time of bonding, but for Kia and Sangita, the excitement fizzled when they saw the movie title—Beauty and the Beast. They slumped into their seats, arms crossed, pouting. "Why couldn't it be a Shah Rukh Khan film?" Sangita muttered under her breath.

"Yeah, I could've watched *Dilwale Dulhania Le Jayenge* for the hundredth time instead," Kia groaned.

As the movie dragged on, the two best friends whispered sarcastic comments to each other, making even the dullest moments hilarious. "Belle should just run away with the teapot," Kia quipped, while Sangita joked, "Forget the Beast, SRK would've swooped in with a helicopter by now!"

Life in the hostel was an endless rollercoaster of bizarre but hilarious moments that would make any outsider wonder if the students were preparing for real life – or a comedy show.

One night, when the mess food was particularly dreadful—watery dal and rice that looked like it had been boiled a week ago—Kia and her friends concocted a plan that would make any master thief proud. "We need real food!" Kia declared, eyeing the dimly lit hostel kitchen. The plan? Steal some onions, tomatoes, and a few green chilies to make their own midnight salad.

They waited until Mr. Pachakili Perumal had made his final rounds and then sneaked into the kitchen like a bunch of ninjas, each girl tiptoeing in perfect synchronization. Rahi, the self-appointed leader of the heist, dramatically signaled for them to "go dark," which was unnecessary given that the lights were already off. Kia, with her typical mischief, started humming the Mission Impossible theme as they made their way to the pantry.

"Shh!" Priyanka hissed as Rahi fumbled with a couple of onions that slipped from her hands and rolled across the floor. Everyone froze momentarily, waiting for the night guard uncle to charge in, but when no footsteps followed, they burst into stifled giggles.

The group managed to escape with a stash of onions, tomatoes, and a lemon. The salad they made wasn't anything fancy—more a random mix of chopped-up vegetables—but in that moment, it felt like the best meal they'd ever had. They sat in a circle on the floor, passing around the bowl as if it were a Michelin-star dish.

Of course, hostel life wasn't just about food heists. Exam preparation holidays brought their own breed of madness. You'd think that exam time would mean books open, highlighters out, and serious studying. But no. For Kia and her gang, "group study" was more a code word for "distraction time."

One lazy afternoon, as they were supposed to be solving math problems, the conversation drifted. "Did you know Dia Ma'am once had a college crush?"

Priyanka blurted out, immediately pulling everyone's attention away from calculus. Within minutes, the group had abandoned the books and was deep in a full-blown discussion about Dia Ma'am's possible love stories. Kia, ever the instigator, started imagining wild tales of love letters hidden in library books, stolen glances during lectures, and secret rendezvous in the chemistry lab.

Hours would fly by, and by the end of the "study session," the only thing they would have discussed in detail was the potential plot of a Bollywood romance. The actual exams? Well, that was a problem for Future Kia.

But the absolute peak of their misadventures came one daring afternoon during exam prep. They'd been craving samosas for days, but there was a strict no-going-outside rule. Desperate times called for desperate measures. Kia, ever the mastermind, came up with a plan so absurd it had to work.

The school bus for day scholars, parked at the back of the hostel, would leave for the market every afternoon. Their idea? Crawl under the side of the bus, James Bond-style, and sneak out to buy samosas from the street vendor. Rahi, always up for a challenge, agreed to go on this ridiculous mission.

The group watched from a distance as Rahi crouched down and shuffled underneath the bus, careful not to be seen by the security guards. They could barely contain their laughter as Rahi, fully committed to her secret-agent persona, inched her way toward freedom. She returned 30 minutes later, victorious, with a brown bag full of samosas held like a trophy.

Rahi dramatically flung the door open, wearing her best 007 smirk, and threw the samosas onto the bed. "For the queen!" she said as if they'd won a major battle. The girls devoured the snacks like they hadn't eaten in weeks, the thrill of getting away with their stunt adding extra flavor to the greasy samosas.

Of course, the next day, Mr. Pachakili Perumal mysteriously knew about their little escapade—whether through hostel gossip or his uncanny sixth sense. He didn't say anything outright but made sure to give Rahi a particularly hard stare during breakfast. The group snickered, knowing they had just narrowly escaped punishment once again.

But perhaps the funniest, most ridiculous moment of their hostel life came one night when Kia's mischievous streak went too far. The group had grown bored with their usual activities and decided to spice things up by pranking Amit—still stuck with his "Kanpur Amit" nickname. They'd noticed that Amit seemed to have a bit of a crush on Kia, so naturally, they decided to capitalize on it.

In the dead of night, they crafted a love letter for Amit, complete with over-the-top romantic lines like "Your eyes are the stars in my universe" and "I wait for the day we can walk hand in hand under the moonlight." Kia cringed as she wrote it but also secretly loved the drama.

They stuck the letter into his schoolbag, and the next day, Amit found it. His reaction was everything they'd hoped for—utter confusion followed by complete panic. He spent the rest of the day looking over his shoulder, afraid he'd been caught in some bizarre romantic conspiracy. Watching from the sidelines, the group could barely hold back their laughter.

Life at the hostel was like this—an endless series of hilarious misadventures, food cravings, absurd study sessions, and moments of pure fun that made the strict rules and academic pressures bearable. Every day brought something new: whether it was plotting to get more contraband food, laughing at ridiculous crushes, or dodging Mr Pachakili Perumal's eagle eyes, Kia and her gang were making memories that would last a lifetime.

And as for the actual studying? Well, that would eventually get done—probably just not before a few more detours into love stories and late-night samosa heists.

Hostel life was full of such moments—bizarre, hilarious, and unforgettable. But amidst the chaos, one thing was certain: Kia and her friends were making memories that would last a lifetime.

CHAPTER 4

THE SÉANCE CIRCLE

One night, as the girls were gathered in their dorm after dinner, Neha brought up the topic of spirits and Ouija boards. Everyone's 12th-grade exams were around the corner, and the stress of studying had started taking a toll. Kia, Rahi, Sangita, Priyanka, and the others huddled together as Neha shared stories of how she could summon spirits.

"Why don't we ask the spirits what questions will come on the exam?" Neha suggested, her eyes twinkling with mischief. Kia, never one to back down from an adventure, was all in. The very idea of asking the supernatural for exam tips was both ridiculous and exciting.

The girls decided to try it out the next night. They gathered the supplies—chart paper, coins, and a white sketch pen—and set up their makeshift Ouija board. The plan? Call Prashant's mom, who had passed away recently, and ask her for some exam guidance. A foolish plan, but in the pressure-cooker environment of exam season, even ghostly advice seemed like a good idea.

At 11:30 p.m., the girls sat in a circle on the school's dark balcony, with flickering candles casting eerie shadows on their faces. The night was unusually still, the only sounds coming from the distant chirping of crickets and the occasional rustle of wind. As they began the ritual, everyone was tense but excited, a nervous energy hanging in the air.

For the first hour, nothing happened. The coin sat motionless in the middle of the board, and Kia started to grow impatient. "This is all nonsense," she declared, pulling her hands away from the coin.

Suddenly, the coin jerked forward.

Everyone froze.

Kia and Neha exchanged wide-eyed glances as the air around them seemed to grow heavy, almost suffocating. Priyanka whispered, "Maybe it's the wind...?" but her shaky voice betrayed her own disbelief.

Kia swallowed hard and leaned back, her hands trembling as they returned to the coin. "Are you Prashant's mom?" Kia asked, her voice barely a whisper. The coin moved slowly, deliberately, sliding over to 'Yes.' Everyone gasped, their hands flying to their mouths.

Rahi, ever the bold one, was quick to ask, "So, uh... what's coming up on the chemistry exam?" She giggled nervously, half-expecting the coin to remain still. But to their shock, the coin slid over to "No."

"No?" Priyanka squeaked. "Does that mean I'm failing?"

The coin slid quickly to "Yes."

The girls burst into laughter despite the eerie atmosphere, the absurdity of the conversation cutting through the tension. "Great, now even spirits think I'm bad at chemistry!" Priyanka moaned, causing more giggles to ripple through the group.

Not to be outdone, Rahi leaned in with a smirk. "Okay, spirit, will Sangita find a boyfriend this year?" she asked, waggling her eyebrows.

The coin zoomed to "No" before any of them could even blink. Sangita threw her hands up in mock defeat, muttering, "Even the afterlife has no hope for me."

But just when the group was ready to dismiss the whole thing as a joke, things took a sinister turn. The air grew colder—noticeably colder. The candles flickered wildly as if caught in a sudden gust of wind, but the night was still. The girls exchanged nervous glances as the coin began moving erratically, jumping from one letter to another, forming incoherent strings of letters.

Kia's heart started pounding in her chest. "Who... who are you?" she stammered, her voice barely audible.

The coin didn't answer the question. Instead, it began spinning faster and faster in circles, making scraping sounds as it slid across the chart paper. The air around them seemed to thrum with a low, vibrating hum. The girls could feel the cold seeping into their bones, and a sense of dread filled the room.

Sangita's voice trembled as she blurted, "I don't think this is Prashant's mom anymore…"

Panic started to rise. Neha, usually the calm one, looked visibly shaken. "I think we should stop," she said, her voice cracking slightly. Kia nodded in agreement, her throat dry. But before they could blow out the candles, the coin jerked violently, throwing itself across the board, landing with a hard thud on the ground.

The girls screamed.

In a frenzy, they blew out the candles, scrambling to get up and leave the dark balcony. As they stumbled into the dorm room, Priyanka looked over her shoulder, half-expecting to see something—someone—following them. But the hallway was empty. The air felt thick, and the eerie silence that followed only added to their fear.

Breathless, they huddled together on one bed, staring at each other with wide eyes. The tension hung in the air like a thick fog. None of them spoke, too terrified to even acknowledge what had just happened.

Rahi, breaking the silence, muttered, "Well, that didn't help us with our chemistry exam."

Everyone burst into nervous laughter, the absurdity of the night finally catching up with them. It was a strange kind of relief—laughter as a way to push back the fear that still lingered in the corners of the room.

The next day, things returned to normal. Or so they thought. Mr. Pachakili Perumal, as usual, caught them sneaking around the balcony, clearly suspicious of their late-night activities. "What were you girls doing there at midnight?" he asked, his voice stern and probing.

Without missing a beat, Kia replied with her trademark smirk, "Just studying, sir."

Mr Perumal gave them a hard look, clearly not buying a word of it, but he let them go with a warning. The girls couldn't help but snicker as they walked away. But deep down, they all knew that something about the previous night had left a mark. It was fun and games—until it wasn't. The spooky encounter, as funny as it was in hindsight, had left them all shaken. Perhaps some things were better left untouched.

Kia and her friends had learned a lesson—albeit a strange one—about meddling with things beyond their control. Their carefree days of pulling pranks and running wild in the hostel were slowly coming to an end, and the looming exams were now all too real. But for now, they laughed it off, making plans for their next big adventure, ready to take on the unknown with humor and a little more caution.

After all, even spirits couldn't resist a little laughter.

CHAPTER 5

CHALK DUST MEMORIES

The final day of high school had arrived, a bittersweet moment that Kia had been dreading and dreaming about for months. It was the day after their class 12 final exams, and the campus, once filled with laughter, pranks, and late-night study sessions, now seemed hauntingly quiet. The realization that this chapter of their lives was closing had finally sunk in.

Kia sat on her bed, staring at the walls of the dormitory that had been her home for the last two years. The room was a mess—half-packed bags, scattered books, and clothes left behind in the rush of exams. But none of that mattered now. What mattered were the people around her, the friends she had made, and the memories they had created. Rahi, Priyanka, Sangita, Neha, and Nishi—they had all become more than just classmates. They were her family away from home.

"Can you believe it's all over?" Rahi's voice broke the silence. She was sitting cross-legged on her bed, scribbling something furiously on a piece of paper. "I feel like we just got here."

Kia smiled softly, but her heart ached. "Yeah, it's crazy. I still remember the first day when Sangita was caught doing that SRK impression," she said, chuckling.

"Hey! I was just warming up for my future acting career," Sangita shot back, her voice filled with mock indignation. "But seriously, what am I going to do without you guys?"

The reality of it all was sinking in. Rahi was heading to Pune for college, while Kia had secured a spot in a prestigious business school in Bangalore. Priyanka was staying back in Kolkata, pursuing economics, and Sangita—well, she was headed to Mumbai, the city of dreams, to follow her passion for Bollywood and acting. Nishi was off to Delhi for engineering. And Neha, their songbird, had chosen to pursue music in Chennai.

It was a scattering of dreams, a web now being stretched across different cities and different futures.

As the afternoon sun began to set, casting long shadows across the dormitory, Kia and her friends gathered one last time. It wasn't like their usual raucous gatherings filled with laughter and jokes. This time, the mood was more subdued, tinged with the weight of goodbyes.

Neha, as always, had her guitar in hand. She strummed softly, the chords filling the room with a melancholic air. Then, with a soft, clear voice, she began to sing *"Mera Kuch Samaan"*. Her voice, hauntingly beautiful, carried the words of the song through the air like a delicate thread, weaving together their shared moments—small pieces of their lives that would soon be memories.

Kia closed her eyes as Neha's voice washed over her, feeling the lump in her throat grow heavier. It wasn't just the song; it was the moment. The realization that this was it—the end of their school days, the end of living together under one roof, sharing secrets, food, and laughter. They would never again be the same group of girls sitting in this dorm, laughing late into the night about silly crushes and stolen vegetables.

When Neha finished singing, the room was thick with emotion. No one said anything for a while. They didn't need to. They knew.

"I wrote something for each of you." Priyanka finally broke the silence, holding up a stack of letters. "Nothing fancy, just... things I never said out loud."

They all followed her lead, pulling out small notes and letters they had written. Kia scribbled a quick message for each of her friends, her words uncharacteristically shaky: "Rahi, stay bold and keep making people laugh.

Priyanka, never stop being the smartest one in the room. Sangita, don't let anyone dull your SRK sparkle. Neha, your voice will change the world."

When they finished writing, they all swapped letters, reading silently as tears slipped down their faces. It wasn't the grand gestures that hit the hardest—it was the raw, simple truths, the memories they had shared.

Then came the shirts. In a last burst of laughter and nostalgia, they pulled out their old school uniforms—white shirts that had seen better days—and handed each other markers. One by one, they signed each other's backs with funny, emotional, and sometimes ridiculous messages.

They laughed through their tears, the sharp contrast of humor and sadness marking the moment as uniquely theirs. The shirts, now filled with memories and inside jokes, would be the keepsakes they would carry with them, a reminder of the friendship that had defined their high school years.

As the sun dipped below the horizon, casting the campus in hues of orange and pink, they ate together one last time. The mess food, though still bad, somehow tasted better. Maybe it was the company. They clicked pictures—too many pictures—trying to capture every fleeting second before they had to go. Kia knew that no picture could ever truly capture what they had, but she took them anyway.

Finally, it was time to leave.

They stood at the gate of the hostel, bags packed, waiting for their respective rides to take them to their next destination. There were no more words left to say. They hugged each other, some holding on a little longer than others. Kia held onto Sangita for a second longer, knowing that this might be the last time they'd be so close.

As Kia climbed into the car that would take her to the train station, she looked back one last time. Her friends and family were standing together, waving through their tears. She waved back, her heart heavy but full.

The campus slowly disappeared from view, but the memories stayed. The laughter, the tears, the pranks, the late-night talks, the stolen food, and the countless adventures – they were all etched in her heart, a part of her that she would carry forever.

As the car sped away, Kia wiped away a tear and smiled. It was the end of an era but the beginning of something new. They were no longer just students of the same school—they were a group of friends bound by memories that would last a lifetime.

And though they were heading in different directions, to different cities and different dreams, Kia knew they would always be connected, no matter where life took them.

CHAPTER 6

TURNING THE PAGE IN BANGALORE

*L*eaving behind the familiar halls of her hostel, Kia boarded the train to Bangalore, her heart full of excitement and apprehension. She was moving to a whole new world—far from home, from her family, and from the friends she had grown up with. The sprawling city of Bangalore awaited her, with its bustling streets, vibrant student life, and endless possibilities.

A dreamy college was everything she had imagined— huge, lively, and teeming with students from every corner of the country. The first day was a blur of introductions, paperwork, and trying to navigate the massive campus. But Kia, being her usual friendly, talkative self, didn't take long to find her groove. She made friends easily, and soon, her laughter could be heard echoing across the dormitory corridors. However, it wasn't long before her carefree nature caught the attention of the seniors.

In particular, one senior stood out: David. With his tall, dark figure, long curly hair, and the effortless charm of a rock star, David was the heartthrob of the college. His deep voice and flawless English made him a magnet for attention. Every girl noticed him, but Kia, being Kia, was oblivious to the chaos her bubbly personality was causing.

Within a week, the dreaded moment arrived— ragging. Kia had heard the whispers in the corridors, the giggles of her classmates who had already been 'welcomed' by their seniors. She had no illusions that her time was coming.

One evening, as she was heading back to her hostel, a group of seniors stopped her. David, naturally, was at the forefront, grinning mischievously. "So, Kia, you're from Assam, right? We're going to give you a very special task tomorrow," he said, his eyes twinkling.

Kia raised an eyebrow, suspicious yet curious. "What kind of task?"

"Oil your hair and come to class like that. Old school style," David smirked.

"With oily hair?" Kia exclaimed, horrified at the thought. "I'll look like a '90s villain!"

"That's the point!" one of the girls from the senior gang chimed in. "And no short dresses allowed for the first term! You freshers have to earn that privilege."

The next morning, Kia showed up to class with oiled hair, looking like a caricature from an old Bollywood movie.

"Kia, you look like you're auditioning for a 70s movie", one of her new friends teased, wiping tears of laughter from her eyes.

"Oh, laugh it up now," Kia grumbled, "your turn is coming."

True to Kia's words, the ragging didn't stop with her. Susan, one of her new friends from class, was made to walk around campus with a placard that said, ***"I love Maths, but Maths hates me"*** for an entire day. Her mortified expressions became the talk of the canteen, and her exaggerated frown won her instant popularity. Susan, on the other hand, was spared no embarrassment either—she was ordered to stand outside the library and deliver a loud Shakespearean monologue to unsuspecting passersby.

Each fresher had their own challenge—some were asked to wear mismatched shoes for an entire week, and others had to sing embarrassing songs in the middle of class. Kia, despite the ragging, found herself laughing harder than ever. It was all done in good fun, and the seniors, although mischievous, made sure never to cross a line.

Amidst all the chaos, the rule about short dresses stayed in place. No matter how fashionable the girls wanted to be, the seniors were adamant—no shorts, skirts, or even capris during the first term. They claimed it was part of the college's 'tradition', though Kia had a sneaking suspicion it was just another form of creative control.

As the weeks passed, Kia started settling into her routine. The ragging, once the source of much trepidation, turned into a series of funny memories she knew she would cherish. There was something oddly bonding about being ordered to do ridiculous tasks by people who, only a year ago, had been in her shoes.

One evening, as they gathered in their hostel rooms, Kia and her new friends recounted their ragging adventures, each story funnier than the last. "Do you think we'll be like this when we're seniors?" Shruti asked, wide-eyed.

"Totally," Susan nodded sagely. "But we'll be nicer."

"Yeah, right," Kia scoffed. "If I get a chance, I'm making the freshers wear clown wigs."

They all burst out laughing, imagining the years ahead. Despite the craziness, the awkward oil partitions, and the weird no-short-dress rule, Kia knew she was going to love this new chapter of her life. The college campus, with all its quirks, was beginning to feel like home.

CHAPTER 7

UNDER THE SENIORS EYE

It had been two weeks since Kia started her classes. She was quickly becoming known as the girl with the most energy, always laughing and talking. One afternoon, as she was hurrying to her economics class, David stopped her in the hallway.

"Hey, you! Wait up!" David called out.

Kia turned around, surprised to see him addressing her directly. "Me?" she asked, pointing to herself.

"Yes, you. What's your name?" David asked, towering over her with a slight smirk.

"Kia... sir," she added nervously, trying to be polite in front of a senior.

"Is it Kia or Sir?" David teased, his smirk widening.

Kia smiled awkwardly. "It's Kia."

"Alright, Kia. I want to see you at CCD at 5 PM today. I need to give you some notes," David said, and before she could respond, he walked away, leaving her flustered.

She had no idea why David, of all people, wanted to see her, but her mind raced with possibilities. Maybe it was just college stuff. Maybe he had noticed her in class? Or perhaps… No, that was silly. Why would someone like David notice someone like her?

CHAPTER 8

A MISSED MEETING

5 PM came and went, and in typical Kia's way, she completely forgot about her meeting with David. It wasn't until later that evening, when she was walking to the hostel, that she saw David again. He was leaning casually against the wall near the cafeteria, and as soon as he saw her, his eyes narrowed.

"Kia!" he called out, stopping her in her tracks.

She hesitated, realizing her mistake. "Yes, sir?" she replied, trying to keep her cool.

"How dare you not come to CCD! I told you to meet me!" David's tone was sharp, and Kia felt a wave of embarrassment wash over her.

"I... I had a motion, sir," Kia stammered, caught off guard by his directness.

'Motion?' David looked at her incredulously, and just as Kia was about to explain her awkward excuse, someone intervened.

"David, leave her alone. Go rag someone else," a calm voice said from behind him.

Kia turned to see James, one of David's friends, walking over with a casual smile. James was different from David—less intense, with soft eyes and a gentle demeanor. His presence instantly made Kia feel more at ease.

David grumbled something under his breath and walked away, leaving Kia standing there with James.

"Don't worry about him," James said with a grin. "He likes messing with people."

Kia smiled back, feeling a rush of gratitude towards James. And just like that, something sparked between them.

CHAPTER 9

FALLING HEAD OVER HEELS

Kia didn't know exactly when it happened, but soon enough, she found herself head over heels in love with James, her senior at college. He was everything she admired—kind, intelligent, and always attentive. James had a way of making her feel special, even with the simplest of gestures. A smile from him, or the way he helped her out in class, sent her heart racing. His easygoing charm and his ability to connect with everyone, including juniors like her, made him even more irresistible.

But there was a catch—James didn't seem to notice Kia in that way. To him, she was just another friendly face in the college crowd. Determined to change that, Kia crafted a plan. Her first step? Befriending Parul *didi*, one of James' closest friends. Parul *didi* was warm and friendly, and soon enough, they bonded over shared classes and campus gossip.

Through casual chats, Kia managed to steer conversations towards James without raising suspicion. Eventually, Parul handed her the ultimate prize – a small slip of paper with James's email address scribbled on it. It was the key to her next move. Kia's heart raced with excitement, her mind already swirling with ideas.

That night, Kia and her friend Susan sneaked out of the hostel. The thrill of their little adventure added to the excitement of what Kia was about to do. They found a dingy cyber café not far from campus, the kind that was hidden away from the watchful eyes of hostel wardens. Kia was giddy with nerves as she sat down at the computer, her hands shaking slightly as she created an anonymous email account.

"I can't believe you're actually doing this," Susan whispered, her eyes wide with amusement.

Kia grinned nervously. "There's no turning back now."

She began typing out the love letter, her fingers flying over the keyboard. She expressed her admiration for James – his intelligence, his kindness, and the way he always seemed to make her day a little brighter. She did not go overboard, but she made it clear that she had been watching him for a while and hoped that one day, he might see her in the same light.

With one final deep breath, Kia hovered her finger over the "send" button.

"Are you sure about this?" Susan asked with a mischievous smile.

Kia bit her lip and nodded. "It's now or never."

She clicked send, and the email was gone—floating into cyberspace and straight into James's inbox. For a moment, Kia and Susan just sat there, the gravity of what she had done sinking in.

Over the next few days, Kia was a bundle of nerves. Every time she saw James on campus, her stomach flipped, and she quickly looked away. Did he read the email? Did he know it was her? Susan teased her relentlessly, reminding her of the risk she had taken.

One morning, in the college library, Kia found herself sitting just a few seats away from James. He was absorbed in his work, as usual, but there was something different about him that day. He seemed distracted, glancing around the room more than usual. At one point, their eyes met, and Kia felt her cheeks burn. James smiled—a soft, knowing smile—and for a brief moment, she wondered if he had figured it out.

CHAPTER 10

EPIC COLLEGE BASH

*W*eeks had passed since Kia sent that anonymous email to James. Despite the initial excitement and anticipation, she had not heard a single word from him about it. She tried to convince herself that it was no big deal, that maybe he had not even seen the email or simply wasn't interested. But deep down, the uncertainty gnawed at her. She found herself scanning the crowd at the canteen or during lectures, hoping for a sign, a clue that James might have figured out her secret.

As the annual cultural fest approached, the entire campus buzzed with excitement. Kia's College was known for its vibrant fest, with students from various departments showcasing their talents through dance, music, drama, and more. For Kia, it was a perfect distraction from the anxious thoughts swirling in her mind.

She, Parul *didi*, and a few other friends settled in the auditorium, enjoying the lively performances. The energy in the room was electric, with students cheering on their classmates and laughter and chatter filling the air. Kia tried to focus on the stage, but her mind kept wandering back to James.

And then, as if the universe had heard her thoughts, she saw him. James was walking towards her, cutting through the crowd as if he owned the room. Her heart leaped into her throat. She froze, trying to convince herself that he was just passing by, but his gaze was fixed on her.

The moment felt surreal. As James reached her, the noise around them seemed to dim, and all Kia could hear was the pounding of her own heart.

"Kia, right?" James said, stopping in front of her.

Kia's throat went dry. "Uh, yes… hi, James," she replied, trying to sound casual, though she could feel her friends exchanging curious glances beside her.

"I received your email," he said, his expression unreadable.

Kia's heart sank into her stomach. He knows. Oh my God, he knows.

"It was you who wrote it, right?" James continued, leaning slightly towards her, his voice low but clear.

Kia's face turned beet red, and her mind went into overdrive. She could feel the eyes of her friends boring into her, waiting for her response. There was no way out of this one. Or was there?

Think, think! her brain screamed. And then, in the most unplanned, nervous blurt of her life, she said, "Me? No, no… what email? Maybe it was from… Cinderella?"

The second the words left her mouth, she wanted to disappear into the floor. Cinderella? Really, Kia? She cursed herself internally. But it was too late now, as the email ID she created started with Cinderella.

James raised an eyebrow, clearly amused. "Cinderella, huh?" he repeated, the corner of his mouth twitching into a smile. He did not push the matter further, but the look in his eyes told her he wasn't buying her awkward denial. "Right. Well, just wanted to check," he added with a knowing smile before walking away, leaving Kia mortified and in a complete pool of embarrassment.

As soon as James was out of earshot, Parul *didi* burst into laughter. "Cinderella? That's the best you could come up with?"

Kia groaned, burying her face in her hands. "I don't know what happened! It just came out!"

"Oh, I'm never letting you live that down" Susan said, shaking her head with a grin.

For the rest of the cultural fest, Kia couldn't shake off the embarrassment. Every time she thought about James' amused expression, she cringed. And yet, there was a part of her that couldn't help but smile. He hadn't seemed upset or dismissive. If anything, he seemed intrigued.

The next few days after the fest were strange for Kia. James hadn't mentioned the email again, but there was a subtle shift in how he interacted with her. She would catch him looking her way more often, and once or twice, they even exchanged brief smiles in passing. It was as if he knew something but wasn't quite ready to confront it—like they shared a secret.

One afternoon, during a group study session with Parul *didi* and some other friends, Kia's mind wandered back to the moment at the fest. "Do you think he knows it was me?" she asked Parul, trying to sound casual.

Parul smirked, flipping through her notes. "Oh, he definitely knows."

Kia's stomach flipped. "You think?"

"I mean, you did kind of make it obvious with that 'Cinderella' comment," Parul teased, rolling her eyes.

Susan chimed in, "If he wasn't sure before, he definitely is now. But hey, maybe he's into fairy tales."

"Very funny," Kia muttered, throwing a pillow at her.

The following week, an announcement was made about a surprise event during the college fest—a talent show where students could showcase hidden talents. Susan, always the prankster, immediately nudged Kia. "You should enter, maybe do a dramatic reading of your email."

Kia laughed, rolling her eyes. "I think I've embarrassed myself enough."

But as it turned out, the talent show would soon become another memorable moment for Kia, one she wouldn't forget.

The night of the event arrived, and students packed the auditorium. There was singing, dancing, comedy skits, and everything in between. As Kia watched from the audience, enjoying the performances, she noticed something curious—James was one of the judges. He sat at the far end of the panel, chatting with the other judges between acts. And then, as if out of nowhere, during one of the breaks, he grabbed the microphone and cleared his throat.

"Before the next act," he began, his eyes scanning the audience, "I've got a quick story to share."

The crowd went silent, clearly intrigued. Kia's heart started racing.

"A while ago," James continued, "I got this mysterious email. Anonymous. Very sweet, very heartfelt. And it was from... well, let's just say, a modern-day Cinderella."

Kia's jaw dropped. He did not just do that!

Laughter rippled through the crowd, and Kia felt her face turn bright red. Susan and Preeti were doubled over, barely able to contain their amusement.

James smiled, his eyes finding Kia in the crowd, holding her gaze for just a moment before continuing. "Now, I do not know who Cinderella is, but I'm keeping an eye out for her. So, if you're out there, don't lose your glass slipper."

The audience erupted into laughter and cheers, and Kia just shook her head, torn between wanting to hide forever and being completely swept up in the charm of the moment.

One thing was for sure: her story with James was far from over.

CHAPTER 11

THE STRUGGLE TO WIN HIS HEART

Kia's attempts to get closer to James were met with mixed results. She tried everything—showing up at his football matches, helping him with assignments, joining him and his friends for coffee at the local hangout spot. But every time she got close, James would retreat, pulling back into his shell. She had heard from mutual friends that he had been in a serious relationship a few years ago, one that had ended in heartbreak. That was the reason for his guarded nature, his reluctance to open up. But Kia couldn't give up. She knew that beneath the walls he had built, there was a heart that could love again.

One day, after a long study session, Kia mustered the courage to ask him out for a casual dinner.

"Hey, James, are you hungry? There's this new place I've been dying to try. Do you want to come with me?"

James hesitated, glancing up from his book. "I'm not really in the mood to go out tonight, Kia. Maybe another time."

Kia smiled, hiding the disappointment that was slowly becoming all too familiar. "No problem, some other time then" she said, her voice as cheerful as ever. But inside, it felt like another door had closed.

She could sense that James wasn't indifferent to her. There were moments—fleeting, barely noticeable—when his eyes lingered on her a little too long or when he smiled at something she said, only to quickly turn away. It was as if he wanted to let her in, but something held him back.

CHAPTER 12

A TURNING POINT

The shift came on an unexpected day. The college was alive with excitement as the holiday season approached. Christmas was just around the corner, and Kia couldn't wait to spend the festive season with her closest friends before heading home. Among the chatter about gifts and parties, one invite stood out: James had asked a small group of them to his house for Christmas Eve dinner.

The thought of spending the evening at James's family home filled Kia with nervous excitement. There was something about this invitation that felt different. Her heart fluttered with a spark of hope, a feeling that had been growing for weeks now.

When Christmas Eve finally arrived, Kia stood in front of James's house, staring up at the beautiful old home wrapped in glowing fairy lights. The warmth of the holiday spirit filled the air, and Kia couldn't shake the feeling that something special was on the horizon.

Inside, the house was cozy, with a tall Christmas tree glowing softly in the corner, the scent of pine and cinnamon wafting through the air. James's parents greeted Kia warmly, making her feel like she was part of the family. The small gathering buzzed with laughter, the comfort of close friendships wrapping them in a blanket of joy.

Kia found herself surrounded by familiar faces, sharing stories and jokes, but her eyes kept drifting towards James. There was something different about him tonight. He was more relaxed, his usual cool, guarded demeanor replaced by a softness she hadn't seen before. His smile was easy, his laugh genuine, and every time their eyes met, Kia felt a warmth spread through her.

As the evening wound down and the fire crackled softly in the hearth, Kia slipped out onto the balcony to catch a breath of fresh air. The night sky was clear, and the stars twinkled as if they had come out just for this moment. The soft glow of Christmas lights around the house cast a magical glow over the scene.

She was lost in thought when she felt someone step beside her. She didn't need to look to know it was James.

"Hey," he said softly, breaking the stillness of the night.

Kia turned to face him, her heart racing. "Hey," she replied, her voice barely above a whisper.

There was a comfortable silence between them as they leaned on the railing, the crisp winter air wrapping around them like a silent spectator to what was about to unfold.

"You know," James started, his voice low, "I've been thinking a lot lately. About us."

Kia's breath hitched. She had waited so long to hear those words but was still unprepared for the wave of emotion that hit her. She stayed silent, too scared to say anything that might disrupt this moment.

James looked out at the sky for a moment, his expression thoughtful. "I know I've been distant. And… I'm sorry. After everything that happened with my past, I wasn't sure I could let myself feel this way again."

Kia felt her heart twist. She knew something had always held James back, but hearing him say it out loud made it all the more real.

"But you", he continued, turning to face her, his eyes soft yet intense, "you've been there every step of the way. Even when I didn't deserve it."

Kia swallowed hard, her emotions bubbling up, threatening to spill over. "James, I—"

Before she could finish, he reached out and took her hand, sending a shiver down her spine. "Kia, somewhere along the way, you became someone I can't imagine my life without."

The world seemed to freeze. Everything else melted away—just the two of them, standing under the stars, with the weight of their unspoken feelings finally rising to the surface.

"And I don't want to lose you," James said, his voice steady but filled with emotion. "Kia… will you be mine?"

Kia's heart felt like it was about to burst. For so long, she had dreamt of this moment, but now that it was here, it felt like magic. She could barely contain the tears that pricked at the corners of her eyes. Nodding through the flood of emotions, she whispered, "Yes, James. Yes."

In that moment, everything else faded. James gently pulled her into his arms, and their lips met in a soft, tender kiss, one filled with all the love, the tension, and the unspoken words that had been building between them for so long. It wasn't just a kiss—it was a culmination of everything they had been through, a silent promise for everything yet to come.

Later that night, after the glow of the moment had settled, James and Kia found themselves back on the balcony, the warmth of their newfound closeness still fresh.

"So," James said, his voice playful now, "about that email… you know, the one from Cinderella?"

Kia groaned, burying her face in her hands. "Oh no, not this again!"

James chuckled, nudging her gently. "Come on, I need to know. Why Cinderella?"

Kia peeked at him through her fingers, her face still flushed from the memory of that embarrassing moment. "It just came out, okay? I panicked!"

James laughed, his eyes twinkling with amusement. "Well, for what it's worth, I'm glad you sent that email. Even if it was from 'Cinderella'."

Kia rolled her eyes, but she couldn't hide her smile. "Well, it worked out in the end, didn't it?"

James nodded, his expression softening again. "Yeah... it did."

They stood there, wrapped in the warmth of the moment, the stars twinkling above them as if the universe was smiling down at them, blessing this turning point in their lives. This was more than just a Christmas Eve dinner—it was the start of something beautiful, something they both knew would change them forever.

Back inside, their friends were celebrating, laughter and joy filling the room. Parul, Susan, and the others were oblivious to the quiet moment that had just unfolded on the balcony, but Kia didn't mind. This moment, this turning point was something she would cherish forever.

As they all gathered around the fireplace, someone suggested a game of Secret Santa. Kia and James exchanged knowing smiles from across the room, their secret now sealed with the warmth of a kiss under the Christmas lights. It was the beginning of a new chapter filled with love, friendship, and the promise of something even more beautiful on the horizon.

CHAPTER 13

DREAMS OF FOREVER

After that magical Christmas Eve, Kia felt as if she was living in a dream. Everything seemed brighter, the world around her humming with a new kind of energy, one that came from the simple joy of being in love. James had become her universe, and every moment they spent together felt like it was filled with stardust.

In the weeks that followed, Kia and James grew inseparable. They spent their mornings walking to class together, their fingers brushing against each other as they laughed and joked about everything from professors to weekend plans. During lunch breaks, they would escape the bustling campus to their favorite café—a little nook tucked away from the world where they could sit for hours, sharing secrets over cups of steaming coffee.

Every evening felt like a celebration as if their love had wrapped them in a cocoon of happiness. James would meet Kia after her classes, and they would stroll through the city streets, lost in conversations about everything under the sun. It was during these walks that their dreams began to take shape. They would talk about the future, not as a distant, abstract thing, but as something that felt within reach—something they were building together.

"I want to travel the world with you," James would say, his eyes lighting up as he imagined their adventures. "Paris, Rome, New York—everywhere. Just us and a couple of backpacks."

Kia would giggle, teasing him about his lack of practicality. "And where do you think we're going to get the money for all these trips?"

James would shrug with a grin. "We'll figure it out. As long as we're together, nothing else matters."

But their dreams were not just about travel. There were quieter, more intimate dreams too—of a life spent building a home together, a family filled with laughter and love. Kia could picture it so clearly: a cozy house with a garden where they would spend lazy Sundays reading, cooking together, and creating a space that was all their own. She imagined holiday dinners, their kids running around, and the two of them sharing knowing smiles from across the room.

One evening, as they lay on the grass in a nearby park, staring up at the stars, James took her hand in his, tracing circles on her palm.

"Kia," he said softly, his voice filled with tenderness that made her heart melt, "have you ever thought about forever?"

Kia turned her head to look at him, her breath catching at the vulnerability in his eyes. "Forever?" she repeated, her voice barely a whisper.

"Yeah," James said, smiling that slow, sweet smile she had fallen in love with. "Like, us. Building a life together. I know it's early, and I don't have everything figured out yet, but when I think about the future… I just can't imagine it without you in it."

Her heart swelled at his words, a warmth flooding her chest. "James," she whispered, squeezing his hand, "I think about it all the time."

They lay there in comfortable silence, the stars twinkling above them like tiny witnesses to the promises they were making without saying a word. At that moment, Kia felt something shift in her heart—something deep and lasting. It wasn't just love anymore. It was a sense of certainty, of knowing that she had found her person.

Of course, no love story is without its bumps along the way. Kia and James had their share of arguments— some silly, others more serious. There were moments of insecurity and doubts that crept in during the quiet hours when they questioned whether they were really ready for this kind of commitment. But what made their relationship special was that they never let those moments define them.

One evening, after a particularly heated argument about their future plans—James wanted to move abroad for work after college, while Kia felt torn about leaving her family behind—they sat on opposite ends of the couch, the tension thick between them.

"I just don't understand why you're not excited about this," James said, frustration lacing his voice. "It's a once-in-a-lifetime opportunity."

Kia bit her lip, trying to find the right words. "It's not that I'm not excited, James. It's just… it's a big change. And I'm scared. I'm scared of losing everything we have here, of leaving behind the people we love."

For a moment, they were silent, both caught in their own thoughts. But then, as always, James moved closer, reaching for her hand.

"Hey," he said softly, his voice gentler now, "I get it. And I don't want to force you into anything you're not ready for. We'll figure it out together, okay? We always do."

Kia looked up at him, her heart swelling with love all over again. "Okay", she whispered, leaning into him, the tension between them melting away.

It was moments like these that reminded them why they worked so well together. They weren't perfect, but they always found their way back to each other, no matter how difficult the road got.

As the months passed, their bond only grew stronger. They made new memories—trips to the beach, late-night movie marathons, and surprise dates that James planned just to see Kia smile. He would show up outside her hostel with flowers for no reason at all or take her on long drives through the quiet street, park by a lake, and talk for hours about their dreams, their fears, and everything in between.

But it wasn't just the big, romantic gestures that made Kia fall deeper in love with him. It was the small moments—the way he would tuck her hair behind her ear when the wind blew it into her face, the way he remembered all the little things she liked, or how he'd quietly hold her hand in the middle of a crowded room, grounding her in his presence.

In the quiet moments when they were alone together, Kia sometimes found herself marveling at how much her life had changed. The girl who had once fumbled her way through crushes and heartbreaks had found something real, something lasting.

James was her partner, her best friend, and the love of her life. And as they stood on the cusp of their future, hand in hand, Kia knew one thing for sure: they were building a forever that would stand the test of time.

In James, she had found not just love but a home.

CHAPTER 14

WHEN DREAMS
FALL APART

The Christmas lights that adorned the streets of Bangalore gleamed like scattered stars, casting their warmth onto the bustling crowds. Kia could feel the festive spirit around her—the smell of cinnamon in the air, the distant sound of carolers, the laughter of families preparing for a night of celebration. But none of it compared to the joy in her heart. This Christmas wasn't just another holiday; it marked three years of love with James. Three years of building a life together, of shared dreams, stolen kisses, and promises whispered under the stars. She thought this love would last forever.

Kia could barely contain her excitement as she drove towards James's house, the small velvet box in her purse carrying the gift she had saved for months—a watch he'd admired during one of their late-night strolls. Her heart fluttered, recalling how he'd held her hand that night, his eyes full of love. He'd been acting strangely these past few weeks, nervous and distant, yet always tender, as if something big was coming. A proposal, maybe? Kia had a feeling that tonight would change their lives forever.

It was just after 6 pm when she pulled up to his house, carefully balancing the cake she had picked up in one hand and a bottle of wine in the other. Her pulse quickened in anticipation of the evening ahead—the music, the laughter, the warmth of James's family, and the promise of a future together. But as she neared the house, the festive warmth she had imagined was nowhere to be found.

The house was dark. The windows, usually glowing with Christmas lights, stood cold and silent. A knot of unease tightened in her chest as she noticed the group of people gathered on the front lawn, their faces pale and stricken with grief.

The air felt heavy, too still, too quiet.

Her steps faltered, the cake wobbling in her trembling hands as her gaze landed on something she had never expected to see: an ambulance parked in front of the house. Its lights flashed red and blue, illuminating the street in a garish blur of color.

Her heart stopped.

The bottle slipped from her grasp, shattering on the pavement with a deafening crash. She barely noticed.

Her eyes were fixed on the paramedics near the door, their faces somber as they loaded a stretcher into the back of the ambulance. A stretcher draped with a white sheet.

"No..." The word left her lips in a breathless whisper, her feet moving of their own accord towards the scene unfolding before her.

Her body felt like it was moving through water, heavy, slow, disbelieving. This couldn't be real. She was supposed to be here for Christmas, for love, for celebration. Not this. Not... this.

As she drew closer, the world around her blurred, fading into a fog of dread. The air grew colder, the festive hum of the city muted as the sound of her heartbeat thundered in her ears.

And then she saw it.

A pair of sneakers peeked out from under the white sheet. These were the familiar sneakers James wore almost every day, the ones she had playfully teased him about for being too old and worn.

Kia's breath hitched in her throat. The cake fell from her hands, crashing onto the pavement in a smear of frosting and broken dreams.

"James?" Her voice cracked, a tremor of disbelief lacing every syllable as she stumbled toward the paramedics.

One of them—a man with kind, tired eyes—stepped forward, gently placing a hand on her shoulder. "I'm sorry, miss," he said quietly, his voice thick with sorrow. "There was an accident. He didn't make it."

The words slammed into her like a freight train, knocking the wind out of her lungs. Kia's knees buckled, and she collapsed onto the pavement, her entire world unraveling in an instant.

"No... no, no, no, this isn't happening..." Her voice broke, the denial spilling from her lips as sobs wracked her body. She couldn't breathe. She couldn't think. All she could see was the lifeless form beneath that cold, unforgiving sheet.

This couldn't be real. It couldn't be James. They had plans and dreams. He was supposed to be waiting for her, with that teasing smile and arms ready to pull her into a warm embrace.

"James!" she cried out, her voice a raw, desperate plea as she reached for the stretcher, her fingers trembling. "Please, no..."

The paramedics exchanged solemn glances but said nothing. They couldn't. There was nothing left to say.

As they lifted the stretcher, something in James's hand caught her eye—a small object clutched tightly in his fingers. Kia's breath stuttered as she reached out, prying open his stiff, cold hand. Inside was a small velvet box.

Her hands shook violently as she opened it, revealing a delicate ring. A ring meant for her.

The sobs tore through her chest, her body shaking as she cradled the box to her heart. James had been on his way to propose, to ask her to spend forever with him. He had been planning their future, the life they were supposed to build together—only to have it stolen from them in a single moment.

"James…" she whispered, her voice broken, choked with grief. "You were supposed to be mine forever…"

Tears streamed down her face as she clutched the ring tighter, her heart splintering with each passing second. The paramedics gently lifted the stretcher into the ambulance, the doors closing with a soft thud.

And then, he was gone.

The man she loved, the man she had built her dreams around, was gone, just like that.

Kia collapsed onto the pavement, her body wracked with sobs as the weight of her loss crushed her chest. She had never imagined this—a world without James, a future without his love. The life they had planned together, the home they were supposed to build—it had all been taken away in an instant.

She stared at the velvet box in her hand, her vision blurred by tears. This was all that was left of their forever.

CHAPTER 15

A VOID WITHIN

Days passed, but for Kia, time had lost all meaning. The bright, vibrant woman who had once lit up every room she entered was gone. In her place was someone else—a shadow of the girl who had once been full of life and love. Her friends tried to reach out, to pull her from the darkness that had consumed her, but it was no use. She had withdrawn into herself, becoming a shell of the person she used to be.

Work, once her passion, had become a chore. She went through the motions, reporting stories with a hollow detachment, never feeling the thrill, she once did. Her colleagues whispered about the change in her, about how she had gone from being the brightest star in the meeting room to someone they barely recognized. But no one dared to bring it up. They all knew about James, and they respected her need for space, even as they watched her spiral deeper into despair.

In those quiet moments, Kia would sometimes catch a glimpse of the person she used to be. She could almost hear her own laughter echoing in the corners of her mind, a sweet reminder of a joy that felt so far away. But every time she tried to grasp it, it slipped through her fingers like sand.

The Kia, who once loved pranks and mischievous fun, had disappeared. In her place was someone who barely spoke, who avoided eye contact, and who recoiled from anything that resembled happiness. She stopped joining her friends for coffee dates, opting instead to sit alone in her dimly lit apartment, the curtains drawn tight against the world outside. Even the vibrant colors of the city seemed muted to her now as if they reflected her own emotional desolation.

One day, as her friends gathered at a café to celebrate a birthday, they sent her countless messages, begging her to join. "Just one hour", they pleaded, their words filled with concern. But Kia sat on her couch, staring blankly at the wall, feeling a heaviness in her chest that made it impossible to move. Instead of bright laughter, she heard only silence. She picked up her phone, ready to type a response, but the words wouldn't come. Instead, she deleted their messages and let the silence envelop her once more.

Even when she did venture out, she found herself lost in a haze. At the grocery store, she wandered the aisles aimlessly, forgetting what she had come for. A mother with a young child passed by, and Kia felt a pang in her heart. The child's laughter was a stark reminder of the future she had envisioned with James—of family and shared moments that would never come to be. Her eyes stung with unshed tears as she quickly turned away, the thought of happiness feeling like a betrayal to his memory.

One evening, while sitting by the window, Kia's gaze fell on a couple walking hand in hand beneath the streetlights. Their joy felt like a knife to her heart, twisting and turning as she remembered how it felt to hold James close, to share the little things that made life beautiful. She buried her face in her hands, sobs wracking her body as she mourned not just for James but for herself—the girl she used to be, full of dreams and laughter, now replaced by a hollow echo of that vibrant spirit.

Kia had become a stranger to herself, a ghost of the girl she had once been. She no longer recognized the reflection staring back at her in the mirror—the bright eyes were gone, replaced by a dull emptiness. But deep down, beneath the layers of grief, a flicker of hope still remained. The memories of love, laughter, and warmth were still there, buried but not forgotten, waiting for the day when she could find the strength to reclaim her life.

CHAPTER 16

AWAKENING IN THE MOUNTAINS

*E*ight long months had passed since that fateful day, each one blending into the next like a watercolor painting left out in the rain. Kia remained ensnared in her grief, but one unexpected phone call changed everything.

Sangita's voice pierced through the fog of Kia's isolation, filled with warmth and concern. "Kia! It's been forever. I miss you, and I'm worried about you. Please, can we talk?"

Kia hesitated, her heart heavy. But the sincerity in Sangita's tone softened her resolve. "I miss you too, Sangita. I'm... just not the same," Kia confessed, her voice barely a whisper.

"I know," Sangita replied gently. "But I have an idea. Take a trip! Remember how we always talked about visiting Leh Ladakh? Just you and me, riding through those breathtaking mountains?"

The mention of Leh Ladakh sparked something deep within Kia—a flicker of the adventurous spirit she thought she had lost forever. "I always wanted to go there... but I don't think I can do it alone", she admitted, feeling a mix of excitement and fear.

"You can do it, Kia! You've always been brave. I believe in you. Just think of it as a chance to find yourself again. I'll be there in spirit, cheering you on", Sangita encouraged.

Kia pondered the thought for days, and finally, she made the decision. She would travel to Leh Ladakh alone. After weeks of planning, she found herself on her beloved bullet, the wind whipping through her hair as she rode from Bangalore to Delhi. The journey was long and exhausting, but every mile brought her closer to a place she had only dreamed of visiting.

As she arrived in Leh, the landscape transformed into a world of wonder. She marveled at the ancient monasteries that clung to the mountainsides, their prayer flags fluttering like colorful whispers against the clear blue sky. She visited the stunning Pangong Lake, where the water shimmered like liquid sapphire under the midday sun. Kia breathed in the crisp mountain air, feeling a small part of her begin to awaken.

But despite the beauty surrounding her, Kia was still the same—haunted by memories of James that lingered in every corner of her mind. She often found herself staring into the distance, lost in thought, as she wandered through the markets and cafés, engaging with locals who welcomed her with open arms. But every time someone smiled at her or laughed, she felt a pang of emptiness, a reminder of the joy that had once been so abundant in her life.

Finally, she reached Nubra Valley, a place Kia had dreamt of spending time in. The golden sand dunes stretched out before her like a sea of endless possibilities, and the towering mountains loomed protectively in the background. As she sat atop a dune, watching the sun dip below the horizon, she felt a rush of emotions. The vibrant colors painted the sky, and for a brief moment, the beauty of the world around her broke through the thick veil of sorrow.

Kia took a deep breath, closing her eyes as she let the cool breeze wash over her. But even amidst the splendor of Nubra Valley, her heart felt heavy. The realization that she was still grieving, that the shadow of James lingered over her, made the vibrant colors dim just a little.

In that quiet moment, as the sun melted into the horizon, tears welled in Kia's eyes. She missed James more than ever. The world felt impossibly vast and lonely without him beside her. She wished he could have seen this place, shared in the wonder of it all, and laughed at her as she fumbled with her camera, trying to capture the perfect shot.

Suddenly, the warmth of his memory enveloped her like a soft embrace. The laughter they shared, the dreams they spoke of—it all felt so vivid, yet so painfully out of reach. She reached for her phone, scrolling through the countless pictures they had taken together. Each one brought a fresh wave of emotion, the laughter echoing in her mind.

As night fell and the stars began to twinkle overhead, Kia felt a mixture of sadness and acceptance wash over her. She could still feel James's presence in the beauty of the mountains, in the crisp air, and in the laughter of the locals who danced and sang around campfires nearby.

Kia knew that her journey was far from over. The road to healing was long and winding, but as she sat there in Nubra Valley, surrounded by the awe of nature, she felt a flicker of hope. Maybe, just maybe, she could find herself again amidst the breathtaking beauty of the mountains. She closed her eyes and whispered to the wind, "I'll carry you with me, James. Always."

CHAPTER 17

EMBRACING THE WILD SPIRIT

*O*ne evening, while wandering through a small, dusty village, Kia stumbled upon a group of travelers huddled around a bonfire. Their loud and infectious laughter filled the air, breaking through the quietude that had enveloped her for so long. She hesitated at the edge of the group, uncertain whether to join them or retreat into the comfort of her solitude.

"Hey! You!" a voice called out, snapping her from her thoughts.

Kia turned to see a man grinning widely at her from across the fire. He was tall with a well-built frame that spoke of strength and adventure. His long hair danced in the cool mountain breeze, framing a rugged face that bore a warm, inviting smile. The husky timbre of his voice resonated through the air, pulling her closer, even as her heart wrestled with hesitation. Dressed in worn-out cargo pants and a faded T-shirt, he looked like he belonged in the wilderness as if the mountains had shaped him.

"You've been standing there for a while," he said, walking towards her. "If you're planning to join the fun, at least grab a seat!"

Caught off guard by his carefree attitude, Kia blinked. "Oh, I didn't mean to intrude."

The man raised an eyebrow, an amused smile playing on his lips. "Intrude? The mountains belong to everyone. Come on, sit down."

Before she could argue, he led her to the circle, introducing himself as Ram. He handed her a cup of warm butter tea, his eyes twinkling with amusement as he made light-hearted jokes with the other travelers.

Kia couldn't help but feel a spark of warmth spreading through her. Ram was everything she had once been—bubbly, confident, and unafraid to embrace life's unpredictability. Watching him was like looking into a mirror, but the reflection was of her past self—the Kia she used to be.

As the evening wore on, Ram's infectious energy enveloped the group. He shared stories of his adventures across the mountains – his daring treks, encounters with locals, and unexpected challenges. Each tale was filled with the thrill of adventure and a zest for life that Kia had lost.

"Come on, Kia! You look like you need a little excitement!" he declared with a mischievous grin. "Tomorrow, we're going to hike up to a hidden waterfall. It'll be breathtaking, I promise!"

Kia hesitated, a part of her wanting to retreat into her cocoon of solitude, but another part—a small flicker of the old Kia—was intrigued. "I don't know... I haven't hiked in a while", she murmured, but the excitement in Ram's eyes was hard to resist.

"Don't worry, I'll make sure you don't fall off any cliffs," he teased, earning a round of laughter from the group. "Besides, you seem like the kind of girl who used to lead the pack. I can tell you're just itching to break free."

The words resonated with her, sending a rush of nostalgia flooding back. She remembered the days of leading her friends on spontaneous adventures, of being the one who sparked excitement in others. Ram was bringing back pieces of herself that she thought were forever lost.

The next morning, Kia found herself awake before dawn, the sun barely peeking over the mountains. She took a deep breath, the crisp air filling her lungs, and made her way to where Ram had set up camp. He was already preparing breakfast, his presence radiating a positive aura that made the world feel a little brighter.

"Ready for an adventure?" he asked, his eyes gleaming with anticipation.

With a small nod, Kia felt a smile tug at her lips – a feeling she had almost forgotten. They set off on the hike, the trail winding through stunning landscapes adorned with colorful wildflowers and rugged cliffs. Ram's enthusiasm was infectious; he would pause to point out fascinating plants, share fun facts, and try to make her laugh with his silly impressions of animals. But Kia was lost in her own way.

After hours of hiking, they finally reached the hidden waterfall, a breathtaking cascade of water tumbling over smooth rocks, sparkling in the sunlight. Kia stood in awe, feeling the cool mist on her face as she took it all in.

"See? Wasn't this worth it?" Ram grinned, splashing water in her direction playfully.

"Yes, it really is beautiful" she replied, her heart swelling with emotion. It was a reminder that life still had moments of wonder, even amidst the pain.

Ram's eyes softened as he watched her, and for a moment, the playful banter faded into something deeper. "You have a light in you, Kia. I can see it. It's still there, waiting to shine."

The sincerity in his voice struck a chord within her. Kia realized that perhaps she didn't have to carry the weight of her grief alone. Maybe, just maybe, she could allow herself to feel joy again – if only for a moment.

As they settled by the waterfall, sharing stories and laughter, Kia felt a piece of herself coming back to life. Ram was like a breath of fresh air, reminding her of the wild spirit she once had. With every splash of water, every shared smile, and every burst of laughter, Kia felt the old Kia—the vibrant, adventurous girl—beginning to emerge from the shadows.

And while she knew the journey to healing was still long, she felt the warmth of hope begin to flicker anew, ignited by the unexpected friendship she had found in the mountains.

CHAPTER 18

A BREATH OF FRESH AIR

In the days that followed, Ram seemed to be everywhere. Whether it was on a trek through the mountains, in the market bartering for fruit, or by the river with his camera slung over his shoulder, his presence was impossible to ignore. He had an infectious energy that made people gravitate towards him, and Kia found herself drawn into his world, even as she grappled with the shadows of her own.

One evening, as they sat on the banks of the Shyok River, Ram turned to Kia and said, "You know, you're the quietest person I've met on this trip. What's your story?"

Kia glanced at him, unsure how much to share. "I came here to get away from everything. Life, mostly."

Ram chuckled, the sound rich and warm. "A lot of people come to these mountains for that. But you don't strike me as someone who's supposed to be this... serious."

"What do you mean?" she asked, genuinely curious.

"I mean," he said, stretching his legs out and leaning back on his elbows, "you remind me of myself. Or at least, how I used to be before... well, before I lost someone."

The words hung in the air between them, thick with emotion. For a moment, Kia felt a wave of understanding pass between them. Ram wasn't just the carefree traveler he appeared to be; he also carried the weight of loss.

"I lost someone too," Kia finally admitted, her voice barely a whisper.

Ram nodded, not pressing her for more. "I figured. It's funny, isn't it? How life brings us to places like this, searching for answers."

That night, as the sun dipped behind the mountains, Ram invited Kia to witness something magical. "There's a place not too far from here where we can see shooting stars," he said, his eyes alight with excitement. "You'll want to make a wish."

Curiosity piqued, Kia felt a tingle of hope in her heart—a feeling she thought had been extinguished forever. They set off into the night, the air cool and crisp, stars beginning to twinkle above them like distant lanterns.

As they reached a secluded hilltop, Kia's breath caught in her throat. The sky was a vast expanse of shimmering stars, brighter and more beautiful than she had ever seen. Ram spread out a blanket on the grass and gestured for her to sit.

"Look up," he said, pointing towards the heavens. "They're coming!"

Kia watched in awe as shooting stars streaked across the sky, fleeting yet breathtaking. "Make a wish," Ram encouraged, his voice soft and encouraging.

Kia closed her eyes, feeling the weight of the moment. "I wish… I wish I could be like I was before," she whispered, her heart aching with the desire to reclaim the joy she had lost.

"Good wish," Ram replied, a smile playing on his lips. "But it's also okay to just be here, in this moment. Sometimes, our wishes change as we grow."

She turned to him, intrigued. "What do you mean?"

Ram looked thoughtful, his gaze distant. "When I was younger, I lost someone who meant the world to me—my younger brother. He was adventurous, always pushing boundaries and exploring new places. After he died, I didn't know how to live without him. I fell into a darkness that felt all-consuming."

Kia felt the familiar tightness in her chest, but she listened intently, captivated by his honesty.

"It took me years to find my way back," he continued. "I traveled to these mountains searching for solace, but I also found pieces of my brother in the beauty around me. I realized that while the pain of loss is always there, it's the memories that keep us connected. Every time I see a shooting star, I think of him, and I make a wish in his honor."

Kia's heart swelled with emotion, her eyes glistening with unshed tears. Ram's vulnerability was a gift, and for the first time, she felt less alone in her grief.

"Fireflies," Ram said suddenly, his voice brightening. "They're another story worth sharing."

Curiosity danced in her eyes as he continued. "Do you know why fireflies glow?"

Kia shook her head, intrigued.

"They do it to attract a mate, to show their beauty to the world. But what's fascinating is that they only have a short time to live. Their glow is a reminder that even in darkness, they create moments of magic and connection. Just like us."

As they spoke, Ram's words illuminated the dim corners of Kia's heart, gradually warming her soul. They hiked to a nearby clearing, where the air was thick with fireflies dancing like tiny lanterns in the night. The sight was mesmerizing – a beautiful display of nature's brilliance.

"See?" Ram grinned, his laughter echoing through the trees. "Even the fireflies know how to make the most of their time!"

Kia laughed, a sound that felt strange yet beautiful. For the first time in months, the corners of her mouth turned upwards. The joy she had buried deep within her stirred awake, ignited by Ram's passion for life.

"Thank you for this," she said softly, her heart swelling with gratitude. "For reminding me that I can still feel alive."

Ram turned to her, his expression earnest. "You've always been alive, Kia. You just needed to let the light back in. Remember, it's okay to carry the weight of your loss and still embrace the beauty around you."

As they stood together, surrounded by fireflies and shooting stars, Kia felt a flicker of hope igniting within her. The night was a tapestry of memories, laughter, and shared stories—reminders that even amidst the pain, there was beauty waiting to be discovered again.

At that moment, she realized that she didn't have to forget James to find joy. She could carry his memory with her, allowing it to illuminate her path as she stepped forward into a new chapter of her life, hand in hand with the wild spirit of the mountains and the unexpected friendship she had found in Ram.

CHAPTER 19

WHISPERS OF
A DREAM

Kia felt lighter than she had in months. Her journey through Ladakh had not only been a break from her life but a pilgrimage of sorts—a search for the pieces of herself she thought had been lost with James. He would always have a place in her heart, a chapter she would cherish forever, but the heaviness that had once smothered her now felt lifted. Much of that change, she knew, was because of Ram.

Before heading back to Bangalore, she needed to thank him. Ram had been the spark that reignited her spirit, and it felt wrong to leave without a proper goodbye. He had brought her laughter, adventure, and hope when she had long believed such things were no longer possible.

As Kia approached the village where they had met, her heart quickened with anticipation. She could already see the group of travelers gathered by the bonfire, just like that first night. She smiled as the warmth of the firelight flickered against their faces, and without hesitation, she called out, "Ram?"

A figure emerged from the group – a tall, broad-shouldered man with long hair. For a brief moment, Kia felt her heart leap in recognition, but as the figure came closer, her breath caught. This wasn't Ram. He had the same build and the same wild hair, but his face was different. His eyes didn't have that mischievous spark; his smile was polite, unfamiliar.

"Did you call for me?" the man asked, his voice deep but devoid of the warmth she remembered.

Kia blinked, her confusion thickening. "You're Ram?"

He nodded, looking at her with mild curiosity. "Yes, that's me. Do we know each other?"

Her pulse quickened. "No, no. I'm sorry, but… you're not the Ram I met. There was someone else, a man who looked like you, with long hair and this infectious energy. He introduced me to the group. He cooked breakfast and took us to the waterfall. He helped me when I needed it the most."

The group around her exchanged confused glances. The woman with the braided hair frowned, stepping closer. "We've been traveling with this Ram for weeks," she said gently. "We don't know anyone else by that name."

Kia's throat tightened. "But he was here. I swear he was. We talked about life and loss… he told me about shooting stars, and we watched fireflies together. He wasn't just someone I imagined. He was real."

The travelers stared at her with growing unease. One of them cleared his throat awkwardly, murmuring, "Maybe you're mixing him up with someone else. This is the only Ram we know."

Kia felt a sharp stab of disbelief. No, this couldn't be right. The bonfire, the river, the treks—they were all real. He was real. But as she scanned the faces around her, it was clear that no one else shared her memory. The Ram standing before her shifted uncomfortably, unsure of what to say, and for the first time, Kia wondered if she had been chasing a ghost.

Panic surged through her. She turned away from them, leaving the circle behind, retracing her steps to every place she and Ram had visited. The waterfall trail, where he'd convinced her to climb higher, laughing the whole way; the riverbank, where they had sat in silence under the stars, talking about life and love; the firefly meadow where he'd told her the story of their survival, their fight to shine even in the darkest moments. Each place seemed empty now, the laughter they'd shared gone, like whispers in the wind.

Where was he?

The deeper she searched, the more elusive the answers became. By the time she reached Nubra Valley, where she and Ram had watched the stars together, her heart felt heavy with doubt. She sat down in the same spot where they had once gazed at the heavens, confusion swirling in her mind. Who was Ram? How could someone so vivid, so full of life, vanish without a trace?

She closed her eyes, exhaling deeply, trying to quiet her thoughts. Perhaps it had all been a dream. Perhaps Ram was nothing more than a figment of her imagination—a creation of her mind in a desperate bid to heal.

Or perhaps…

A soft breeze brushed against her skin, and Kia opened her eyes. To her surprise, Ram was sitting beside her, just as he had been before, his familiar smile lighting up the night.

"You're still searching for answers," he said, his voice as gentle as the wind. "But sometimes, the answers aren't what matters. It's the journey that changes you."

Kia stared at him, her heart pounding in her chest. "But... were you real? Or just a dream?"

Ram smiled, a twinkle in his eye. "Does it matter? You found what you needed, didn't you?"

She couldn't deny it. She had found healing, a way back to herself. But the uncertainty gnawed at her. "I don't understand. How could you have been here, and no one remembers you?"

Ram leaned back, gazing up at the stars. "People like me and James... we come into your life when you need us. Not always to stay but to remind you of something you've forgotten. It doesn't matter whether I was real or not, Kia. What matters is that you rediscovered yourself."

Kia felt tears pricking at her eyes. "But you helped me so much... how can I let go of that?"

He turned to her, his gaze soft but steady. "You don't have to let go. I'll always be here. So will James. We're part of you now. But you need to move forward. You need to love yourself enough to keep going, to find joy again."

She swallowed hard, trying to absorb his words. "Will I ever see you again?"

Ram's smile grew wistful. "In different ways, at different times. But you don't need to search for me. Focus on loving yourself. People like me come and go, but your own light is what matters."

As he spoke, the stars above them seemed to shimmer brighter, and when Kia blinked, Ram was gone. The breeze whispered through the valley, and Kia sat alone, gazing up at the heavens. She could feel his presence still, not as a man beside her, but as a memory, a guide, a part of her journey.

Was Ram real? Was he a dream? The question lingered, but as Kia rose to leave, she realized it didn't matter whether real or imagined, Ram had given her the strength to move forward.

And with James in her heart, and the lessons of Ram in her soul, Kia was ready to embrace whatever life held next.

Life's challenges may momentarily dim our light, but they cannot extinguish it. We hold the power to reignite our spirits, to seek joy, and to love again—because life, despite its trials, is a beautiful tapestry woven with love, laughter, and the promise of tomorrow.

CONCLUSION

THE RESILIENT THREAD OF LIFE

*L*ife has an uncanny way of throwing curveballs at us, doesn't it? Kia's journey mirrors the experiences many of us have faced—those moments when everything we believed to be true is suddenly swept away. It was James's death that altered the course of her life, pulling her into the depths of grief that seemed unshakable. In Kia's heartbreak, we see our own: the loss of loved ones, the end of relationships, the collapse of dreams that once seemed so certain.

For a long time, Kia lost herself in the shadows of what could have been, much like we often do when confronted with overwhelming loss. The laughter, the joy, and the vibrant energy she once carried seemed like distant memories. And yet, life, in its own mysterious way, continued to beckon her forward.

Kia's journey through Ladakh—the lonely rides, the fleeting encounters, and her mysterious connection with Ram—was more than just a trip. It was the beginning of her healing, a path back to herself. Ram, whether real or imagined, became the symbol of hope she needed. His words and the adventures they shared reminded her that life isn't about holding on to the past but learning to live with its echoes. The fireflies they watched together, flickering in the dark, were a metaphor for her own resilience—how, even in the darkness, we can find our light again.

But this story isn't just about Kia. It's about all of us because life, in its unpredictability, will always present challenges. There will be moments when we feel lost, where we wonder if we will ever find our way back to the people we once were. There will be loves that stay with us long after they've gone and dreams that we have to let go. But as Kia's journey teaches us, we never truly lose ourselves.

Love transforms and evolves—whether it's for someone who's passed on or for someone we've left behind—but it never truly vanishes. The memories remain, shaping us in ways we may not understand, but they don't define us. Kia found her way forward, not by forgetting James or the pain she endured, but by accepting that loss is a part of the human experience.

Kia's return to her life, her friends, and the laughter she once embraced is a reminder that life, despite its hardships, continues to call us towards new beginnings. We may not always have the answers, and the people we meet—like Ram—may leave us with more questions than clarity, but the lesson is the same: life is about moving forward, even when it feels impossible.

As Kia learned, the human spirit is more resilient than we give it credit for. We are all capable of finding joy in the little moments, cherishing the relationships we still have, and embracing the future, even when the past feels like a weight on our shoulders. In the end, Kia's story is our story—a reminder that while life may not always be what we planned, it is always worth living.

As Kia sat under the stars in Nubra Valley, it wasn't just Ram or James she saw—it was herself. And in that moment, she understood that love, life, and loss are all part of the same beautiful, unpredictable tapestry. We can't always control what happens, but we can choose how we move forward, carrying the memories of those we've loved while allowing ourselves to love again.